Hoping for a Home After Nigeria

CRABTREE
PUBLISHING COMPANY
WWW.CRABTREEBOOKS.COM

Heather C. Hudak

CRABTREE
PUBLISHING COMPANY
WWW.CRABTREEBOOKS.COM

Author: Heather C. Hudak

Editors: Sarah Eason, Harriet McGregor, and Janine Deschenes

Proofreader and indexer: Wendy Scavuzzo

Editorial director: Kathy Middleton

Design: Paul Myerscough and Jessica Moon

Photo research: Rachel Blount

Production coordinator and Prepress technician: Ken Wright

Print coordinator: Katherine Berti

Consultant: Hawa Sabriye

Written, developed, and produced by Calcium

Publisher's Note: The story presented in this book is a fictional account based on extensive research of real-life accounts by refugees, with the aim of reflecting the true experience of refugee children and their families.

Photo Credits:
t=Top, c=Center, b=Bottom, l= Left, r=Right

Cover: Getty: Jane Sweeney

Inside: Jessica Moon: p. 29b; Shutterstock: Koldunova Anna: p. 1l; Andrii Bezvershenko: p. 3; Bmszealand: pp. 6b, 9c, 10-11c, 17t; Jordi C: pp. 5r, 6t, 26-27c; ComicVector703: p. 24b; Bumble Dee: p. 14b; Elenabsl: p. 17b; Great Vector Elements: p. 23r; Helga Khorimarko: p. 16t; Cindy Lee: p. 27t; Lorimer Images: p. 16c; Loveshop: p. 5l; Lydia: p. 21b; Macrovector: p. 24t; Modamo: p. 15; Mspoint: p. 28t; Paschal Okwara: p. 7t; Oleg525: p. 22t; OzturkUmit: p. 12t; Panda Vector: p. 20t; Photoroyalty: p. 9tr; Onigbinde Raphael: p. 8; StreetVJ: pp. 22c, 22b, 23t; Sudowoodo: p. 5t, 29t; Sugiyarto: p. 1bg; Tayvay: p. 12r; VectorShots: p. 7c; Werezuu: p. 26bl; What's My Name: p. 19r; © UNHCR: © UNHCR/Xavier Bourgois: pp. 11t, 13l; © UNHCR/Hélène Caux: pp. 14t, 18b, 19t; © UNHCR/Romain Desclous: pp. 10-11b; © UNHCR/Rahima Gambo: pp. 18t, 28b; Wikimedia Commons: Shiraz Chakera: p. 20c; DFID - UK Department for International Development: pp. 26-27b, 29c; DonCamillo: p 25; Clinton Ugboke: p. 24r.

Library and Archives Canada Cataloguing in Publication

Title: Hoping for a home after Nigeria / Heather C. Hudak.
Names: Hudak, Heather C., 1975- author.
Series: Leaving my homeland: after the journey.
Description: Series statement: Leaving my homeland: after the journey | Includes index.
Identifiers: Canadiana (print) 20190114916 | Canadiana (ebook) 20190114932 | ISBN 9780778765028 (softcover) | ISBN 9780778764960 (hardcover) | ISBN 9781427123763 (HTML)
Subjects: LCSH: Refugees—Nigeria—Juvenile literature. | LCSH: Refugee children—Nigeria—Juvenile literature. | LCSH: Refugees—Social conditions—Juvenile literature. | LCSH: Nigeria—History—1993—Juvenile literature. | LCSH: Nigeria—Social conditions—Juvenile literature.
Classification: LCC HV640.5.A3 H83 2019 | DDC j305.23086/91409669—dc23

Library of Congress Cataloging-in-Publication Data

Names: Hudak, Heather C., 1975- author.
Title: Hoping for a home after Nigeria / Heather C. Hudak.
Description: New York : Crabtree Publishing Company, [2019] | Series: Leaving my homeland: after the journey | Includes index.
Identifiers: LCCN 2019023040 (print) | LCCN 2019023041 (ebook) | ISBN 9780778764960 (hardback) | ISBN 9780778765028 (paperback) | ISBN 9781427123763 (ebook)
Subjects: LCSH: Refugees--Nigeria--Juvenile literature. | Refugee children--Nigeria--Juvenile literature.
Classification: LCC HV640.5.A3 H83 2019 (print) | LCC HV640.5.A3 (ebook) | DDC 362.7/791409669--dc23
LC record available at https://lccn.loc.gov/2019023040
LC ebook record available at https://lccn.loc.gov/2019023041

Crabtree Publishing Company

www.crabtreebooks.com   1-800-387-7650

Printed in the U.S.A./082019/CG20190712

Published in Canada
Crabtree Publishing
616 Welland Ave.
St. Catharines, Ontario
L2M 5V6

Published in the United States
Crabtree Publishing
PMB 59051
350 Fifth Avenue, 59th Floor
New York, New York 10118

Published in the United Kingdom
Crabtree Publishing
Maritime House
Basin Road North, Hove
BN41 1WR

Published in Australia
Crabtree Publishing
Unit 3 – 5 Currumbin Court
Capalaba
QLD 4157

What Is in This Book?

Baseema's Story: Fleeing Nigeria

Hi! My name is Baseema. I live in Kano, a city in northwest Nigeria. I love shopping at the market with my mother, then cooking a meal for my family with the fresh foods we buy. I have a nice life here, but it was not always like this. My family moved to Kano about a year ago. It was a long and dangerous journey to get here.

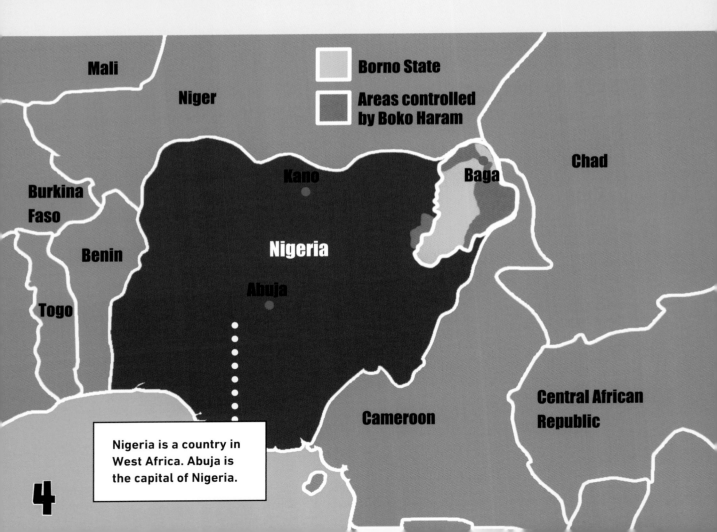

Mali

Niger

Burkina
Faso

Benin

Togo

Borno State

Areas controlled
by Boko Haram

Kano

Baga

Chad

Nigeria

Abuja

Cameroon

Central African
Republic

Nigeria is a country in
West Africa. Abuja is
the capital of Nigeria.

A child's family has the responsibility to help ensure the child's **rights** are protected and help them learn to stand up for their rights. While you read through this book, think about these rights.

Nigeria's flag

Boko Haram has attacked many villages in Borno State. It kidnaps girls to be wives for its soldiers, and to cook and clean for them.

*I grew up in a village called Baga in Borno State. A violent **terrorist** group named Boko Haram is very active in this area. They destroy villages and hurt people. One day, when I was 13 years old, my worst nightmare came true. My cousin heard Boko Haram motorcycles. They were coming to our village. We just ran. We fled to Maiduguri where my father was working.*

My father's business friend said we could live with them in Maiduguri. We stayed for a few years, but then Boko Haram began to attack our community there, and we knew we had to move on. We are much safer in Kano, and my family is all together now.

My Homeland, Nigeria

More than 200 million people live in Nigeria. About 62 percent live in extreme **poverty**. That is more than any other country in the world. Today, conflict in Nigeria affects more than 8.5 million people. The fighting is between Boko Haram and government **security forces**. It has put many people at risk, causing a **humanitarian crisis**.

People living in extreme poverty do not have access to proper shelter, toilets, and other basic services.

Boko Haram is most active in Borno State. The group believes in an extreme form of Islam, and wants people to follow its beliefs. Most **Muslims** do not agree with this. The group began to attack the police and the government in 2009. Over the years, their attacks have become more deadly and take place more often. Thousands of people have been killed in the fighting. The government has tried to stop Boko Haram. But there is no end in sight.

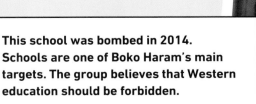

This school was bombed in 2014. Schools are one of Boko Haram's main targets. The group believes that Western education should be forbidden.

These children are internally displaced persons (IDPs). They live in an IDP camp in Abuja, which is Nigeria's capital city. Some IDPs have lived there for many years.

More than 2.5 million people have fled their homes. They want to find a safe place to live. There are more than 2 million IDPs living in Nigeria. Most live in communities that have offered to take them in. Others live in camps. There are also more than 271,990 Nigerian **refugees** in other countries.

Baseema's Story: Leaving My Homeland

Three years have passed since I left my home in Baga. Each day, I see stories in the newspaper about more villages being attacked. They bring back terrible memories for me. At first, Boko Haram mainly targeted the police and the army. Then, they started to attack schools. The people in our village began to fear Boko Haram would attack us. They closed the school. My sister Nafisaa and I had to study at home instead. My father said we could not leave the house.

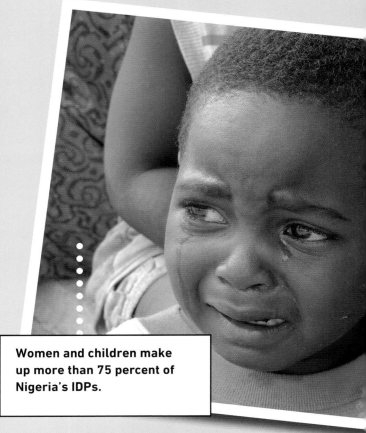

Women and children make up more than 75 percent of Nigeria's IDPs.

My father was on a business trip in Maiduguri when Boko Haram attacked our village. It was just my mother, my aunt, and my sister, Nafisaa, and I. After we fled our house, we walked for days. We cried for joy when we came to a village. My mother had not slept for more than a few hours since we started our journey. She stayed on the lookout for danger. She was in pain because her feet were covered in cuts. She had not had any time to put on shoes. The villagers helped clean and bandage her feet, but my mother still has scars on them.

You have the right to be protected from being hurt and mistreated, in body or mind.

One of the first Boko Haram attacks on a school took place at Success International Private School in Maiduguri on July 29, 2009. Six classrooms and an office were destroyed.

My cousin and his family were already at the village. They had escaped in a small truck. They hoped to find us so we could travel to the city of Maiduguri together. The drive to Maiduguri took a long time. There is only one safe road into the city. It is often closed due to Boko Haram attacks. I can still remember how it felt to have my father's arms around me when we first saw each other again.

Baga

Maiduguri

Borno State

Baga is a village near Lake Chad in Borno State. It is about 120 miles (193 km) from Maiduguri.

Searching for Safety

Millions of IDPs have fled to Maiduguri from nearby towns and villages. Maiduguri is the capital city of Borno State. But this has put a huge strain on the city. The population has more than doubled since 2009. The city cannot cope. There is not enough food and clean water for everyone. Health care services are scarce, and many people cannot find places to live. But many IDPs have no other place to go. Their homes and villages have been destroyed. They often live with their hosts for many years.

Five or six families often live under the same roof. There can be as many as 80 people sharing the same small space. Host families often struggle. They cannot support themselves and their guests. It costs a lot of money to feed and shelter so many people.

These girls are at school in an IDP camp in Maiduguri. In many northern parts of Nigeria, more than 50 percent of women aged 15 to 24 have never gone to school.

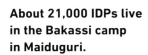

About 21,000 IDPs live in the Bakassi camp in Maiduguri.

These Nigerian refugees have crossed the country's border and hope to find safety in Cameroon.

Not all IDPs have a place to live when they arrive in Maiduguri. Many live in camps. Others rely on the kindness of strangers. In some places, landowners have let IDPs build shelters on their property. But the conditions in these places are poor. IDPs do not always have access to clean water. There may be no proper toilets or ways to get rid of waste. Diseases can spread quickly in these places. Some IDPs even die.

Many IDPs were farmers. They are now unable to farm their fields. This has led to food shortages in Maiduguri. The price of food has more than tripled. Some people even cook grass just so they have something to eat.

Baseema's Story: Living in Maiduguri

I miss living in Baga. My family had a nice home. We had room for our whole family, as well as a few guests. Our house was always filled with laughter. Life was good before Boko Haram arrived.

Maiduguri is very different from Baga. Many of the people in and around Baga farmed or fished for a living. Few people in Maiduguri are farmers. They work in offices, banks, and stores. Many people cannot find work at all. Back home, my father was a farmer until his father died. Then, he took over his father's role as one of the leaders of our community. But our community is gone. In Maiduguri, father left the house early each morning to look for work. Sometimes, his old business contacts had work for him, but it was not steady work.

Boko Haram attacks have forced many families to abandon their farms and animals in rural Nigeria.

Story in Numbers

More than

98 percent

of IDPs want to return to their homes. Around

76 percent

of them say they cannot do so until the government improves security in the villages.

Dear Jameelaa,
I cannot believe three years have passed since the attack. It is hard living with strangers. The house is too small for all of us. When we first got to Maiduguri, I felt safe. But soon, the newspapers were filled with stories of Boko Haram. They attacked places across the city. Father would not let Nafisaa and I go out alone very often. We want to join you in Kano, but we need to save money to make the trip. I am glad things are a little better in Maiduguri now. Boko Haram is not as active as they once were. But I am sad to see stories about attacks in other parts of Borno State. Love, Baseema

Over two days in early 2019, more than 30,000 people fled from Rann, Nigeria, to Goura, Cameroon, to escape Boko Haram attacks.

We wanted to pay toward our household, but we had very little money. To make up for it, my mother helped clean the house, cook, and care for the younger children. Our hosts took in another family, too. There were 20 of us living in one small house.

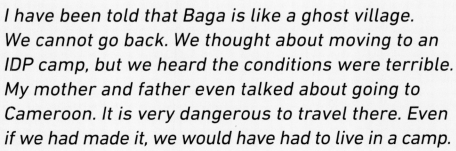

I have been told that Baga is like a ghost village. We cannot go back. We thought about moving to an IDP camp, but we heard the conditions were terrible. My mother and father even talked about going to Cameroon. It is very dangerous to travel there. Even if we had made it, we would have had to live in a camp.

Continuing Conflict

Before the fighting, Maiduguri was a thriving city. It was an important **trade** and education center for northern Nigeria. The city has an airport and some of the best universities and hospitals in the country. People come from all over to work and study in Maiduguri. Today, the city is at risk of falling under the control of Boko Haram.

Maiduguri is a gateway to northern Nigeria. This means it has links to other towns and cities in the area. Boko Haram took over five of the six highways that lead to the city. The group bombed bridges along the five highways. This kept people from getting in and out of Maiduguri. The government closed the highways for several years because of the attacks. Today, they are still closed at times, and are not safe to travel.

Yerwa is the original name of the city of Maiduguri. Yerwa is derived from a word that means "promising or blessed land."

Boko Haram sometimes pretend to be soldiers so that they can attack vehicles traveling along the highways to and from Maiduguri.

Boko Haram have attacked and killed drivers on busy highways in other cities, too, such as Kano.

The only usable highway from Maiduguri is to the city of Damaturu. The government controls this highway, for now. But Boko Haram still attacks towns along the route. Security forces must work hard to keep the highway open.

If Boko Haram take over the last highway, the people of Maiduguri will have no way out of the city by land. They would be cut off from the rest of the country. If this happens, Boko Haram could take control of Maiduguri and the rest of Borno State. That would be extremely dangerous for the people that live there.

Baseema's Story: Fear and Hope

The government reopened some schools. I was so excited to go to school. Sitting at home all day was boring. I remember the day my father brought home my new school uniform and book bag. He was so proud. I could not wait to use them.

Keeping up with schoolwork was difficult at first. It had been so long since I went to school. Soon, I made many new friends. Most of them were IDPs, too. One of the girls told me how she was taken from her bed one night. Boko Haram **enslaved** her for nearly three years. She was beaten every day. She had to cook and clean for them. After a long time, the Nigerian army freed her. I cannot imagine the horror.

About 28 percent of Nigerian children aged 7 to 14 go to school and also work to help support their families.

Story in Numbers

Not all schools have reopened in Nigeria. About

10.5 million
children still are not in school. Almost

2,300
teachers have been killed by Boko Haram.

Teachers are supposed to use only the local language in Nigerian schools. But most textbooks in Nigeria are written in English. Teachers often use a mix of both languages to help students learn.

Nafisaa did not go back to school. At 19 years old, she felt she was too old to return. Instead, she started a small business. She bought some dried flowers and mixed them with water to make a drink called zobo. She bought empty bottles and filled them with the drink. Then she sold them. She made enough money to pay for my brother, Abdullah, to go back to university. Nafisaa had more happy news—she announced she was engaged to be married!

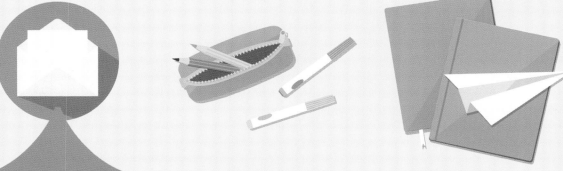

Dear Jameelaa,
I remember how excited I was to go back to school. But I was also afraid. I had heard so many stories of girls being kidnapped from schools. My school worked hard to keep us safe. They even had their own police. Sometimes, **counselors** came to our school. They talked to us about our fears. I always felt better after I talked to them. Love, Baseema

17

Living Conditions

The Nigerian government and the **United Nations High Commissioner for Refugees (UNHCR)** help IDPs. The UNHCR provides protection, shelter, and other services to more than 432,000 IDPs. The government tries to stop Boko Haram. However, it does not have a proper program to help IDPs caught up in the crisis.

Many Nigerians do not have access to health care and education. In the northeast, Boko Haram has attacked health care centers and workers. In **host communities** and camps, schools are overcrowded. There are not enough supplies for all students. It is hard for **humanitarian groups** to send workers to Nigeria. There is too much violence. Because Boko Haram controls many roads, some parts of the country cannot be reached at all.

Nigeria has more children aged 6 to 11 out of school than any other country in the world.

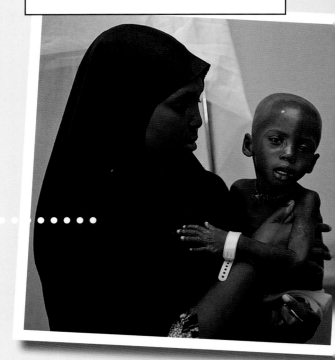

About 2.5 million children suffer from malnutrition in Nigeria. Few get the help they need.

18

These UNHCR workers are bringing emergency supplies to IDPs sheltering in the Bakassi camp.

More Nigerians are malnourished now than ever before. More than 5.2 million people do not have enough food. **Aid** workers try to get food to as many people as they can.

The government relies on support from humanitarian groups to help the IDPs. The United Nations World Food Programme (WFP) is a humanitarian group. It helps IDPs sign up for aid programs. One program gives IDPs money. They can buy one food basket each month with the money. CARE is a humanitarian group that aims to end poverty. In Nigeria, the group hopes to help 900,000 people. It provides food, water, shelter, farming supplies, and other items.

Story in Numbers

About

$1.1 billion

is needed to provide aid to Nigerians. Only about

21 percent

of these funds have been raised so far.

Baseema's Story: Leaving Maiduguri

Just when I began to feel settled in Maiduguri, life turned upside-down again. My father was on his way to our **mosque** when a bomb went off inside. He was hit by some flying rocks and was cut all over his arms and legs. Some of his friends were inside the mosque, and they died. The week before, a bomb went off at a local market. It killed nearly 20 people. We knew we could not stay in Maiduguri.

We decided to finally go to Kano. My brother, Umar, was there. He worked as an **engineer** with an oil company. It is a good job, and he was able to find a house that would have enough room for our family. I was so excited to see Jameelaa. She lived there, too, with her husband and their daughter. She was expecting another child. I had not seen Jameelaa in years.

Kano is the second-largest city in Nigeria. From Dala Hill, it is possible to see much of the city below.

UN Rights of the Child

You have the right to choose your own friends, and to join or set up groups, as long as it is not harmful to others.

20

Dear Umar,

I am sad that Nafisaa will not be coming with us to live with you and that you were not able to be here for her wedding. She wore a beautiful dress. We had more food than I have seen in years. Now, she lives with her husband and his family. I will miss her when we leave. We have been through so much together, but she is happy. I cannot wait to live with you in Kano. We are so grateful for your help. Love, Baseema

In Nigeria, weddings are a festive time when two families become one. People wear bright colors, dance, and eat a lot of food.

Abdullah and I took over Nafisaa's business when she got married. We needed money to buy bus tickets. We knew if we worked hard, we could save enough in a few weeks. A bombing near our home almost ruined our plan. We were put under a **curfew** for a few days. We could not sell any zobo. I was worried about how long it would take to make up for the lost sales. But, thankfully, when the curfew was lifted, we had more sales than ever.

Life in Kano

Kano is the capital city of Kano State. The city is home to around 3.6 million people. The bus journey from Maiduguri to Kano takes between six and seven hours. It involves passing through security **checkpoints**. If there are attacks from Boko Haram along the way, buses change their route. This can make the journey much slower.

Companies make many products in Kano, such as foods, fabric, steel, and trucks. The city has large markets. Buyers and sellers travel there from all over Nigeria and West Africa to do business. The main **industry** is groundnut farming. Groundnuts are peanut-like crops. They are sent from Nigeria to countries around the world.

This is the Kofar Mata Dye Pit in Kano. Fabric is dyed here before it is sold.

People have lived in the Kano area for more than 1,000 years.

Kano Central Mosque is one of the largest mosques in the country.

However, industries in Kano are not as successful as they once were. This is because Boko Haram is still a threat and attacks by the group still sometimes take place. For example, about 120 people were killed and 260 injured in the 2014 bombing of the Kano Central Mosque. Attacks like this have left people frightened and anxious, and less likely to carry out their normal day-to-day activities. The city's businesses have suffered as a result.

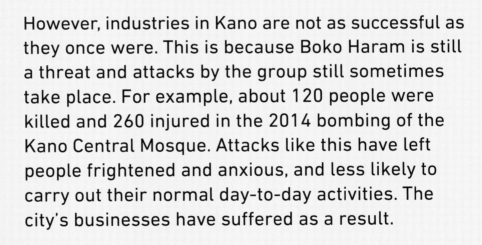

The leader of Kano has talked about turning local mosques into schools. Boko Haram targets young boys who are not in school. They hope the boys will join them. Using mosques as schools would provide education for boys, and help stop the spread of Boko Haram.

Baseema's Story: Reunited at Last

On the way to Kano, I saw the ruins of small villages and towns. All that was left were burned out cars and crumbling buildings. The people had all gone to find safety. We were so happy to finally see Umar and my Aunt Dalmaa waiting for us in Kano.

We were all very tired from our long journey, but we could not wait to see our new home. We made a special stop along the way to see Jameelaa. I was so excited to finally meet my niece. She was so beautiful and sweet. Jameelaa told me to place my hand on her belly to feel the baby kicking inside. It gave me such hope for the future of our family.

This Nigerian woman is selling groundnuts. They are a good source of protein.

Story in Numbers

There are believed to be more than

11 million

people living in Kano State.

24

Dear Nafisaa,
I love finding out all about Kano. The Durbar Festival is amazing. It happens each year to mark the end of **Ramadan**. It starts with Muslim prayers, then there is a parade. Men ride through the streets on horseback while musicians play. It is very exciting to see. One day, Father took me to Gidan Makama Museum. It was so cool! The building was made in the 1400s. It has many arts, crafts, and historic items. I learned so much. I hope you are safe. I wish you could be here with us.
Love, Baseema

Nigerians have celebrated the Durbar Festival for more than 500 years. It was first used by fighters to show off their skills before going to war.

Dalmaa and Umar had found a house in the Old City. It has enough room for all of us to live comfortably. It is nice to have a home of our own again.

We are close to Kurmi Market. I go there often with my mother and Jameelaa. We buy bread, vegetables, and spices for our dinner. We like to look at the wood and leather handicrafts sold there. There are many artists in Kano. My mother is a talented weaver. She hopes to one day sell her goods at the market. Father is looking for work, too. Abdullah has found work at a groundnut farm. He is taking more classes part time at Bayero University. Life in Kano is much better for us.

Baseema's Story: An Uncertain Future

We have been in Kano for more than a year now. I feel safer here than I did in Maiduguri. But it does not feel like home. I am not sure I will ever feel the same way about Kano as I did about Baga. I think about it often. I wonder what happened to the people. Will I ever see them again?

The people of Kano have been very kind and welcoming. Most are **Hausa**, like us. I remember when we first moved into our house. The neighbors brought us dinner that night. They were quite poor, but they had more than us. They wanted to share what they could. We do the same for new people when they arrive. That is the Kano way.

Some IDPs hope to rebuild in other parts of Nigeria that have been less affected by Boko Haram, such as Akure.

A British government program has helped 7,000 girls and women in northern Nigeria train as health workers. They will use their new skills to help save the lives of thousands of mothers, babies, and children.

Dear Baseema,
Your father sent me a letter last month. He said you will soon finish high school. We are very proud of you. Your aunt and I would love for you to come to visit us in the United States. We have plenty of room. We would love to show you around. If you like it here, we would be happy for you to stay. You could apply to go to university here and build a new life where you are safe and have many opportunities.
Best regards, your kawun (uncle)

For now, we still live with Umar. He will soon get married. We are saving money to get a place of our own. We would like to host families like ours. Abdullah works full time now, and his earnings help us a lot.

I will finish high school soon. Not many girls complete high school in Nigeria. My parents have always believed in my education. They wanted me to have the best chance in life. For now, I hope to find a job at the groundnut plant where my brother works. I will do anything I can to help my family get a home of our own where we can feel safe and happy.

27

Do Not Forget Our Stories!

The Nigerian army works hard to keep Boko Haram from taking more ground. As a result, the group is not as strong as it once was. Its attacks on Maiduguri were at their worst between 2013 and 2015. But it still controls villages in the area around Lake Chad. Kidnappings and attacks are still common.

In 2018, at least 1,200 people were killed in Boko Haram attacks. Around 200,000 people became IDPs. However, fighting has lessened in places, and people there have returned home. But damage to the area makes it difficult to get food, water, and health care to many people. In 2019, fighting in the north became worse again leading up to the **elections**. Boko Haram wanted to disrupt the election and keep people from getting to the polls to vote.

The Future Prowess Islamic Foundation provides a safe place for orphans and IDP children. Hundreds of students go to the school and thousands of others are on a waitlist. These IDP children are cared for by the foundation. They are washing clothes on the banks of the River Gadabul in Maiduguri.

UN Rights of the Child

You have the right to choose your own religion and beliefs. Your parents should help you decide what is right and wrong, and what is best for you.

Life for people in northern Nigeria is still uncertain, but they are hopeful for a better future.

Life is hard for IDPs in northern Nigeria. Still, they work hard to rebuild their lives in their host communities. They hope for a better future. Local communities work together to overcome difficulties. They help one another cope with the **trauma** they have faced. They hope to build a positive future for themselves and their families. It is important to never forget the stories of IDPs living in Nigeria and around the world.

Discussion Prompts

1. What does Boko Haram hope to achieve?
2. Why are people forced to flee their homes?
3. What kinds of support are available for IDPs in Nigeria?

Glossary

aid Help or support

checkpoints Barriers where checks are carried out

counselors People who give advice about personal problems

curfew A rule that tells people when they must stay indoors

elections The voting in of a new leader by the people

engineer A person who designs or builds machines, systems, and structures

enslaved Owned by someone else

Hausa One of the three largest ethnic groups in Nigeria

host communities Places that offer to give IDPs a home

humanitarian crisis An event that brings harm to the health, safety, and well-being of a large group of people

humanitarian groups Organizations that aim to help people and ease suffering

industry Production of goods or services

internally displaced persons (IDPs) People who are forced from their homes during a conflict but remain in the country

malnutrition Not having the nutrients needed to be healthy

mosque A Muslim place of worship

Muslims People who follow the religion of Islam

poverty The state of being very poor and having few belongings

Ramadan A holy time in which Muslims fast during the hours of daylight

refugees People who flee from their own country to another due to unsafe conditions

rights Privileges and freedoms protected by law

security forces Police or soldiers who provide security or protection

terrorist Using violence to force people to accept a point of view

trade Purchase and sale of goods

trauma A very severe shock or very upsetting experience

United Nations High Commissioner for Refugees (UNHCR) A program that protects and supports refugees everywhere

Learning More

Books

Cantor, Rachel Anne. *Nigeria* (Countries We Come From).
Bearport Publishing, 2017.

Jeffries, Joyce. *Who Are Refugees?* (What's the Issue?). Kidhaven, 2019.

Okparanta, Chinelo. *Under the Udala Trees*. Mariner Books, 2016.

Seavey, Lura Rogers. *Nigeria* (Enchantment of the World).
Children's Press, 2016.

Websites

https://www.cia.gov/library/publications/the-world-factbook/geos/ni.html
Find out about the people, history, culture, and economy of Nigeria.

https://nigeria.savethechildren.net
Discover what Save the Children is doing to help children in Nigeria.

www.unhcr.org/nigeria-emergency.html
Get the facts about the UNHCR's work in Nigeria.

www.unicef.org/rightsite/files/uncrcchilldfriendlylanguage.pdf
Read about the UN Convention on the Rights of the Child.

Index

About the Author

Heather C. Hudak travels all over the world and loves to learn about different cultures. She has been to more than 50 countries, from Brazil to Indonesia and loads of others in between. When she is not on the road, she enjoys spending time with her husband and many rescue pets.